P9-AOI-669

Jochen Weeber
Illustrated by Fariba Gholizadeh

What in the World Is Wrong with GISBERT?

Louisville, Kentucky

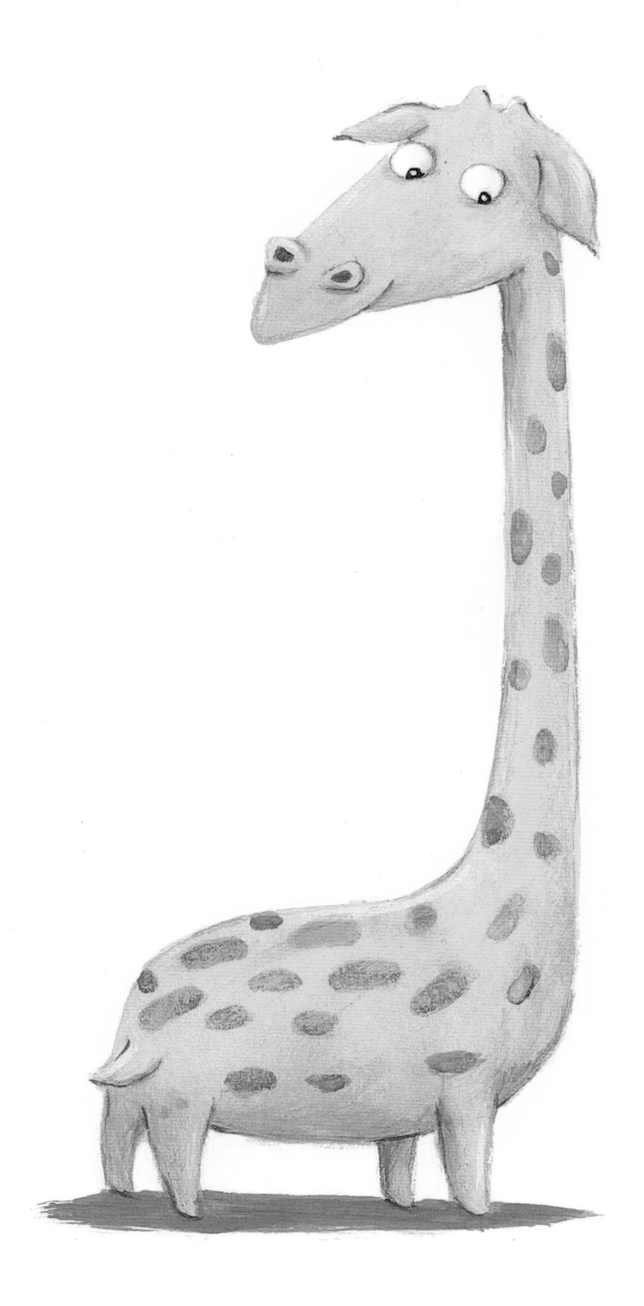

Gisbert was a tall, young giraffe.
He was tall enough to do everything
a giraffe might want to do.

He watched TV.

He played with
his friends.

"My life is very good,"
he thought, as he
closed his eyes
for a nap in the trees.

But then one day something changed.
On his way to kindergarten on Monday, he heard two hyenas whispering, "Look at his brown spots!"

They laughed and exclaimed,
“They are all over him. That looks funny!”

Suddenly, Gisbert felt something strange happen:
He was shrinking! A whole two inches!
No one else could see it, but he could!

In music class on Tuesday, he was learning a new marching song on the trumpet. He had some trouble with the song and messed up a few of the notes. All the others dropped their instruments and covered their ears.

"Oh boy, that sounds awful!" the hippo said.

Gisbert felt it clearly: He was shrinking again. A whole six inches! No one else could see it, but he could.

“Are you all right?” asked his parents that evening.

“I’m fine,” he said, but inside he thought, *I don’t know what’s going on.*

At the playground on Wednesday, it happened again.
Two giggling ostriches raced past him and shouted,
“Move along, beanpole!”

Gisbert felt it clearly: He was shrinking again.
A whole ten inches! No one else could see it, but he could.

That night he stood in front of the mirror.
The shrinking seemed to be unstoppable!

His parents noticed that he wasn't feeling well.

"What has upset you?" they asked, worried.

"I'm fine," he said, but inside he thought,
I don't know what's going on.

In gymnastics class on Thursday, he tried to hang
from the climbing pole for the first time in his life.
It took all his courage to try. He stood on the gym mat,
concentrating, when he heard the apes whisper,
“He’d better not try. Giraffes can’t do that. He’ll fall!”

Gisbert felt it clearly: He was shrinking again.
A foot this time! No one else could see it, but he could.

"Is there something we can help you with?" his parents asked him that evening.

"I'm fine," he said, but inside he thought, *I don't know what's going on.*

At the swimming pool on Friday, things didn't go any better. Gisbert really wanted to try the new slide, but everything went wrong. He was so tall he got stuck on one of the curves!

"Watch out—blockade!" the lion shouted. Everyone laughed. It was quite some time before somebody could rescue him.

Gisbert felt it clearly: He was shrinking again. Two whole feet! No one else could see it, but he could.

"Are you still not feeling better, Gisbert?" asked his parents that evening. He could tell they were concerned.

"I'm fine," he said, but inside he thought, *I don't know what's going on.*

On the playground on Saturday, Gisbert wanted to join his friends in the playhouse. “I’ve shrunk so much this week,” he thought, “so I won’t take up much space.”

But the others said, “You don’t fit in here, Gisbert!”

Gisbert felt it clearly: He was shrinking again. Two more feet! No one else could see it, but he could.

“We are very worried about you, Gisbert,” said his parents that evening.

Gisbert crept under the sofa.

“I’m fine,” he said, but inside he thought, *I don’t know what’s going on.*

On Sunday he
felt so sad.
And so small.

Nothing
seemed to
be much
fun to him
anymore.

Gisbert stayed home from school the
whole next week. His mother hugged him,
and his father tickled him between the horns.
But nothing seemed to cheer him up.

Then one day, his friends left a small present on his doorstep.

“Come back to school,” the note read. “We miss you!”

Slowly he started feeling better. That night when his parents asked if he was OK, he said, “Now I know what’s going on!”

Gisbert told his parents everything that had happened.

“Their words made me feel like I was shrinking,” he said. “And the smaller I got, the worse I felt. But it’s not bad to be tall or small. Meerkats are small. So are mice and ants. But I felt so weak and sad.”

“Sometimes people say things that hurt you, even if they don’t mean to,” his mother said. “It’s okay to tell them that their words made you sad.”

“And you can always talk to us, Gisbert,” his father added.

When they were done talking, Gisbert felt much better.

The very next day, Gisbert went to the playground again.

“Hey, look, there’s Gisbert!” the hippo shouted.

“It’s great to have you back!” the lion roared.

The others nodded. “Join us in the playhouse,” they said. “It’s going to rain soon.”

The ape reached out for Gisbert’s hand, and he joined his friends.

“We all missed you,”
his friends said.

“Our orchestra sounds boring without you,” the hippo said.

“We can’t cross the river without you,” the lion added.

“We’re sorry that our words made you sad, Gisbert,” they all said. “We didn’t mean to do that.”

“By the way,” the hyena added, “you look really cute with those spots.”

Gisbert looked at his friends.
All of a sudden, he felt something happening. It started in his feet and spread all over him. A cozy, warm feeling, as if the sun was shining inside of him.

Nobody suspected that something was about to happen. Not even Gisbert.
But then . . .

He burst through the roof!

Everybody laughed and laughed. Gisbert was tall again! He'd grown a whole six feet in half a second.

And everyone could see!

For Nele and Romy

Jochen Weeber
is an author, poet, and musician in Reutinger, Germany.

Fariba Gholizadeh
was born in Iran and studied graphic design in Tehran and in Mainz, Germany.

© 2016 Schwabenverlag AG, Patmos Verlag, Ostfildern (Germany)

Original title: *Was ist bloss mit Gisbert los?*

This edition published 2018 in the United States of America by Flyaway Books, 100 Witherspoon Street, Louisville, Kentucky 40202-1396. Online at www.flyawaybooks.com.

18 19 20 21 22 23 24 25 26 27—10 9 8 7 6 5 4 3 2 1

All rights reserved. No part of this book may be reproduced or transmitted in any form or by any means, electronic or mechanical, including photocopying, recording, or by any information storage or retrieval system, without permission in writing from the publisher. For information, address Flyaway Books, 100 Witherspoon Street, Louisville, Kentucky 40202-1396. Or contact us online at www.flyawaybooks.com.

Design by Finken & Bumiller, Stuttgart, Germany

Library of Congress Cataloging-in-Publication Data
Names: Weeber, Jochen, author.
Title: What in the world is wrong with Gisbert? / Jochen Weeber ; illustrated by Fariba Gholizadeh.
Other titles: Was ist bloss mit Gisbert los? English
Description: Louisville, Kentucky : Flyaway Books, 2018.
Identifiers: LCCN 2018002945 | ISBN 9781947888029 (hbk. : alk. paper)
Subjects: LCSH: Self-esteem--Religious aspects--Christianity--Juvenile literature. | Bullying--Religious aspects--Christianity--Juvenile literature. | Giraffes--Juvenile literature.
Classification: LCC BV4598.24 .W4413 2018 | DDC 242--dc23
LC record available at https://lccn.loc.gov/2018002945

PRINTED IN CHINA

Most Flyaway Books are available at special quantity discounts when purchased in bulk by corporations, organizations, and special-interest groups. For more information, please e-mail SpecialSales@flyawaybooks.com.

WITHDRAWN